The Great **BIG** Sleep

For my darling Debbie,
part Bear, part Squirrel x

THE GREAT BIG SLEEP
A RED FOX BOOK 978 1 849 41988 8
Published in Great Britain by Red Fox,
an imprint of Random House Children's Publishers UK
A Random House Group Company, This edition published 2016
1 3 5 7 9 10 8 6 4 2
Copyright © Sean Julian, 2016
Red Fox Books are published by Random House Children's Publishers UK,
61–63 Uxbridge Road, London W5 5SA
www.randomhousechildrens.co.uk
www.randomhouse.co.uk
Addresses for companies within The Random House Group Limited
can be found at: www.randomhouse.co.uk/offices.htm, THE RANDOM
HOUSE GROUP Limited Reg. No. 954009. A CIP catalogue record for
this book is available from the British Library.
Printed in China

Sean Julian

The Great BIG Sleep

RED FOX

Winter had begun, and Squirrel and Bear
were getting ready for the Great Big Sleep.

"Have you got enough food there?" laughed Bear,
as Squirrel shovelled more nuts onto his plate.
"Almost," replied Squirrel. "Just a little more!"

"Well, eat up," said Bear. "It's nearly time for bed."
But Squirrel wasn't feeling tired at all.

Through the window, Squirrel could see the forest covered in a blanket of crisp white snow. "Maybe we could have one last play in the snow before we go to sleep?" he suggested.

So Squirrel and Bear went outside to make snow animals and throw snowballs.

Bear was the perfect sledge, but soon he was feeling sleepy.

"I think I'm ready for my Great Big Sleep," he yawned.
But Squirrel didn't feel sleepy in the slightest.
"Let's have some warm milk," said Bear.

Once they had wiped away their white, milky moustaches, Bear's eyes were starting to feel very heavy. But Squirrel's eyes were bright – he was wide awake. "What about reading a bedtime story?" suggested Bear.

So they read one story. And then another. "Could we have one more story?" asked Squirrel.

"I'm sorry, Squirrel, but I'm just too tired," said Bear.
"Do you think if you tried you could get to sleep?"
Squirrel jumped into his bed. "I'll try my best."
"Sleep tight," Bear whispered.

But although Squirrel tried, he still wasn't sleepy.

Crunch! Crunch! Crunch!

"*More* nuts?" asked Bear, amazed that Squirrel could still be hungry. "I thought that a few more would help me doze off," Squirrel replied.

VROOOM VROOOM VROOOM

"Just hoovering up all the crumbs," shouted Squirrel over the noise.

Slurrrrp Slurrrrp Slurrrrp

"Just having one more drink," said Squirrel, before taking another big slurp.

Squirrel tried everything he could to make himself sleepy,
but all he managed to do was keep Bear awake.

Bear got more and more cross . . .

And when Squirrel decided
to practise his trumpet it
was the last straw.

"Be quiet!" roared the tired and grumpy bear. "Go to sleep!!!"

Squirrel felt bad for making Bear so cross, but he just wasn't sleepy. He crept out of the den so he wouldn't disturb Bear any more.

Squirrel
bounced,

and slid

and hopped in the fluffy
white snow, down to the
frozen lake.

He sat and watched as the animals danced and played on the ice. But he didn't notice the snow beginning to fall harder and the night growing colder.

Meanwhile, the den was so quiet that Bear couldn't sleep because he was worried. Where was Squirrel?

Bear lit his lantern and headed out into
the snow to search for him.

The snow was heavy and had covered all Squirrel's tracks.
Bear didn't know how he would ever find his friend!

He looked here . . .

there . . .

and everywhere!

He called out for his friend, but there was no reply. "What have I done?" Bear sobbed, slumping down in the snow. "Squirrel is lost for ever, all because I was horrid and grumpy!"

But then, in the distance, Bear heard a funny noise . . .

He followed the noise through the snow, and at last he found a little squirrel-shaped snow animal with very noisy, chattering teeth.

CHATTER CHATTER CHATTER

It was Squirrel!

After shaking all the snow off Squirrel, Bear snuggled him
into his fur and carried him home through the cold night.

"Don't you worry, Squirrel,"
he whispered to his shivering friend.
"I'll soon have you home by the fire."

Bear wrapped Squirrel up in a scarf and sat him
by the fire until he thawed out.
"I'm sorry, Bear," sobbed Squirrel. "I didn't mean
to cause all this trouble."

"That's OK, Squirrel," smiled Bear. "I'm sorry I snapped at you.
I was tired and grumpy, but I didn't mean to upset you."

"I'm feeling a little tired myself," said Squirrel with a yawn.
"I think I might finally be ready for my Great Big Sleep."

And AT LAST Squirrel fell into a lovely deep sleep. Squirrel's snores were a little bit noisy, but Bear didn't mind too much. He was just happy that his friend was safe.

And before he knew it, Bear was fast asleep too.

Bear woke up to the sweet smell of spring.
He yawned and stretched, got up and made
a delicious breakfast to share with Squirrel.

But Squirrel just kept on snoring and snoozing. He slept all morning.
Bear didn't know what to do – he was hungry!

And then Bear had an idea . . .

"You had done enough sleeping," laughed Bear,
as he walked with Squirrel through the spring forest.
And that was the end of the Great Big Sleep.